SHORT STORIES

OF

THE PARANORMAL

BY

CANDACE NADINE
BREEN

Copyright © 2022 Candace Nadine Breen

All rights reserved.

ISBN: 9798352755839

Imprint: Independently published

Cover photo: © Canva

No part of this publication may be translated, reproduced or transmitted in any form without prior permission in writing from the author. The author and publisher are not liable for any typographical errors, content mistakes, inaccuracies or omissions related to the information in this book.

Printed in the United States of America.

To all those who believe in the power of magick.

TATON HOUSE

CHAPTER ONE

"You ain't from 'round here, are you?"

She hefted her heavy bags from the trunk of her car. The Mississippi July sun beat down upon her naked brown shoulders. She placed her luggage on the dusty dirt country road and tiredly smiled at the old, overall-clad man riding atop a tractor who stopped to speak to her.

"No sir, I'm not," was the only response she could muster. The old man removed his straw hat, wiping his dark brown face with a kerchief he removed from the pocket of his faded overalls.

"I reckon you weren't. Ain't too many folks want to stay in the Taton House," he said, rolling a strand of straw grass between his full lips.

"Why you stayin'?" he asked, eyeing her suspiciously.

Annoyed and sweaty, she replied, "I'm a writer working on a novel. I need to spend some time away from the city for a bit." She forced a smile for the nosey old man who apparently had decided that he would invade her mental space without even offering to help her with her bags. Considering her for a minute, he climbed down from his beat up tractor.

"I'm the caretaker of Taton House. I know all there is to know 'bout the house: its bones, its history," he paused before continuing for dramatic effect. "and its *hants.*" His hollow eyes bore into her, but she was definitely not afraid of ghosts. She remembered how her grandmother, born in Alabama, used to tell "scary stories" about slave ghosts and haunted houses that once belonged to slave masters and haunted swamps and graves…

"Well, thank you, Mister--" she said, wanting to get away from this old man and his creepy implications.

"--Cummings. Benjamin A. Cummings, at your service," He made a clumsy bow, his damp white hair glistening in the sun. She felt like she was actually melting under the sun's unforgiving rays and she so desperately wanted a drink and to get inside the house, regardless of any supposed "hants".

"Is it always this hot here, Mister Cummings?" she asked, wiping the back of her neck. He paused before answering.

"Yeeeeep," he slowly replied, twirling that piece of straw grass between his teeth. " Best get in the house. Cooler. Always cooler in the house."

"Well, that's a relief," she said, glancing at the house that oddly seemed to flex its outer walls at finally being noticed. "Oh, and my name is Shemikah Robertson." She held out a sweaty hand. Benjamin glanced at her hand with no intention of shaking it.

" 'Taint my practice to shake hands, Miss Robertson, 'specially in the sight of *her*," he whispered, pointing his eyes towards the house.

This guy is a bit off his rocker, Shemikah thought. "Her?" she questioned. Nodding, Benjamin spoke, his voice a whisper yet again.

"A word of advice, Miss Robertson: take care not to walk the floors at night. This here house has some dark stories that come to life in the dark--"

“THANK *you*, Mr. Cummings---” Shemikah cut in.

“Benjamin--” he corrected.

“*Mister* Cummings, thank you, but I’m a big girl. I’ll be fine. Have a nice day.” Shemikah Robertson hauled her luggage up the three steps to the front door on the porch and closed the already open front door on the image of Benjamin A. Cummings.

“Dang city folks,” he muttered, climbing back onto his tractor.

CHAPTER TWO

She hated the Southern heat.The way the dry air soaked the life right out of you. The heat made her skin feel as though she were sitting in a giant dehydrator.

Her publisher said that she needed to spend some time in the country so that she could relax and be able to "open her mind" to new story ideas. Lately, her novels have been as dry as the Mississippi summer heat. This was her last chance to come up with something fresh, interesting, and reader-worthy before her publisher dropped her. She had to go into town, experience Southern life fully, including staying in this historical old house her agent had rented for her in the middle of the country.

This historical house was called Taton House, and it dated back to the 1800s. Shemikah had done some research before arriving here and found that this house once belonged to a Eugene Taton, a well-known and prosperous slave owner. This massive house towered above the ghosts of long gone cotton fields and simple slave houses. Local legend has it that Taton, himself, was a horrible man whose wife died of yellow fever while giving birth. The baby didn't make it. Taton became very bitter after losing both his wife and his stillborn male child. He became enraged every time slaves had children and would say they "had babies like rabbits". It was rumored that he would snatch slave children in the middle of the night by walking into the slave quarters unannounced and demanding that they give up their child or be whipped to death. No one ever knew what happened to the children he took. Some say the children who could walk were sold while the infants were killed and buried somewhere on the property out of sight...some said the babies were drowned in the swamp which also sat on the Taton plantation.

There was one slave, however, who would put an end to Taton's child-snatching. He was called Big Bill, and he came from Ghana. No one but the slave master knew his African name. He had broad shoulders, long, thick legs and dark chocolate skin that had been smoothed by the Southern sun. He was a great worker and could do the same work as three average slaves on the plantation. He was valued, which is why no one crossed him and, sometimes, he was allowed rest breaks that the other slaves were not permitted. With Big Bill on the plantation, Taton was weary of sneaking into slave cabins and stealing children for fear of encountering the intimidating and burly slave.

Many times, Big Bill would sometimes mourn for his home back in Ghana. Before he was a slave in America, he had a beautiful life in Ghana. He remembered his parents and his people. He remembered running freely as a child and he remembered sitting beside his father on cool nights and watching the night sky. The older he became, the fewer memories of his home he remembered. He wanted to know his name. Not what he was called *here,* but what he was called *there*, back home in Ghana. But the slavemaster would have none of that. Taton seemed to enjoy having all the enslaved beaten until very little or nothing remained of their Mother Country–no culture, language, no pride, no spirit. Big Bill was determined to know his real name, and he knew all slavemasters knew all of their enslaved names because they kept books when they captured them so they could keep track of their slave property and change their names to names that made sense to them, slave owners.

Without his name---his African name---he was no one. He had no home. He was like a lost lamb with no direction. If he were to die today, his soul would be lost and could not join his people. Knowing his birth name would allow him to be recognized by his people and he could join them in the great Paradise.

CHAPTER THREE

Big Bill was planning to escape slave life. He had heard of the Underground Railroad and, although he had never heard of the place, he had intended to go all the way to Canada. He, his wife and his son would escape under the cover of darkness to freedom. When the moment came, they wasted no time following the instructions those who worked the Underground railroad gave them. The swamps were dark and uncertain, but Big Bill, his family, and their guides pushed forward. Big Bill's heart was pounding so hard he thought someone would hear it and find him. Big Bill carried his son in his massive arms as he pulled up the rear behind the Underground Railroad guides and his wife. All was going as planned. After so many years of slaving on the Taton plantation, Big Bill and his family would finally be free.

What would freedom be like? he wondered. Would he be an equal to whites? Would he be able to walk the roads and not be harassed, yelled and spat at or referred to as "boy"?

Suddenly, there was a noise behind them. Angry dogs could be heard barking behind them as they ducked into a drainage tunnel. His wife stifled a startled scream and his son started to cry. Handing his son to his wife, Big Bill decided he would fend off the approaching men and their angry dogs.

"Big Bill, don't! You won't make it! They gots guns!" his wife shrieked as their guides silently directed them to keep moving. Grabbing Big Bill's thick arms, his wife pulled him into the tunnel, attempting to push him and encourage him to get in front of her. Sweat and fear gripped his wife as she held her son close to her body. The sounds of panting filled the drainage tunnel.

Big Bill's jaw was set in firm determination. His mind was made up. Big Bill would protect his family, but just as he was about to step out of the drainage tunnel to do battle, he heard his wife running towards him. Before Big Bill could react, she had squeezed her tiny frame between him and the wall of the drainage tunnel and was already outside screaming and waving her arms to grab the attention of the men whose dogs began to snarl and growl at her.

CHAPTER FOUR

She had been captured. She had pushed their son into Big Bill's arms before the men gripped the hem of her dirty dress and pulled her from the tunnel. She fell face down into the mud and grime of the drainage tunnel. Big Bill wanted to save her, but he knew if he went to her, their son would also be captured and would have either killed or sold off to another plantation.

"Big Bill, c'mon! You can't save her," one guide whispered hoarsely. Big Bill knew the guide was right, but he couldn't take his eyes off the frightened face of his wife, the love of his life. She screamed as one man raised an axe over her. Forcing himself to turn away, Big Bill pressed his son into his wide chest, shielding him from the brutal and bloody attack.

Big Bill ran behind the guides just as the man holding the axe smashed it into her back, the crushing sound echoing throughout the tunnel. Her body lay still as her life pooled around her. The men, satisfied that they had injected fear into the runaways, spat on the corpse and disappeared into the night.

X X X

He wanted to go back to her body to hold her one last time as the red life drained from her body, to feel her one last time. They told him they must make haste or they, too, would meet the same fate. There was no time for stopping, but he shoved his son into the arms of one guide and ran back to the body of his wife.

"Big Bill, don't–What *are* you doing?!" another guide shouted. His son cried out and stretched out a tiny arm towards his father.

"Papa, come back!" his son shouted.

Turning towards his son and the guides, Big Bill said in his booming voice, "Take him to freedom! If'n I don't make it, tell 'im his papa 'n mama loved 'im! I ain't gonna let my love lie dead in no ditch! Now, g'wan!" With open mouths, the guides looked at Big Bill, nodded, and swiftly made their way through the tunnel.

CHAPTER FIVE

The men and the dogs were gone. Big Bill rushed to the body of his wife and slid his powerful arms beneath her body.

"Jeanie, you ain't gotta worry no mo' It's all ovah. No mo' strugglin'. No mo' bein' 'fraid." He could feel her body struggling to breathe. She was still alive, but barely. She opened her eyes briefly as blood continued to spread around her broken body.

"Bill---" she whispered.

"Shhhh, you ain't gotsta talk, baby. It's alright. Big Bill here gots you and I's gonna make sho' you is buried right 'n proper."

"Bill," she spoke again, blood trickling from the corners of her mouth. "He---

knows----- your name, your REAL name."

"Baby?"

"Massah Taton-----he knows-----your AFRICAN name." For a moment, anger flared like a flame in Big Bill's wide eyes.

"Jeanie, I sho' does love yah. Now rest yer head and 'llow Big Bill ter take care of yah." Big Bill's eyes began to water as he held his wife in his arms beneath the dark and unforgiving sky.

X X X

True to his word, Big Bill, using only his bare hands, buried his beloved beneath a nearby cypress tree. He had carried her about a mile away from the drainage tunnel, as far away from where she died as possible, but close enough to the escape route they had followed via the Underground Railroad.

"Now, you is free. Can't no massah hurt yah no mo'." With that, Big Bill set his mind on returning to the plantation to avenge his wife's death and to demand that Taton tell him his REAL name.

But Bill Big never got the chance to kill Euguene Taton or ever know his African name. When Big Bill broke into the shed behind the plantation house and stole the largest axe, he could get his hands on. Eugene Taton had already disappeared. None of the other slaves knew where he went or when he left. Some said he left because he feared Big Bill's wrath for sending out those men after them and suspected that the men wouldn't be able to kill Big Bill but could surely kill his wife, son and anyone else who was with them. Others said that Eugene Taton was running from some folks to whom he owed a lot of money. Whatever the reason, Eugene

Taton was gone and with him, Big Bill's vengeance and his African name.

Big Bill knew he could never join his wife until he knew his name. So he stayed on the Taton plantation until the old man returned. Taton's house was still furnished and most of his belongings were still there, as far as Big Bill could tell. It just looked like Eugene had stepped out for a minute. Big Bill knew his son would be safe and also that his son would be a free man one day. The thought of his son experiencing freedom and not having to be whipped and slave to a white man brought joy to Big Bill's heart.

CHAPTER SIX

He knew he should have gone with his son, but he also knew that Taton had to pay for murdering his wife in cold blood. Now that his wife had gone to Paradise, Big Bill had to join her, but he couldn't go into paradise with all his African ancestors if he didn't know his African name. Jeanie knew hers and his soul would never rest until he found out what his was.

Unfortunately, Big Bill would pass on before he could find Ole Man Taton and before he could know what his African name was. Taton never returned to the plantation. Folks said he died of pneumonia from hiding out in the woods in bad weather. The slaves all left after Taton died and headed towards Canada, where they would be free.

There were the dogs again. Big Bill tried to shake the sounds from his head. He would remain haunted by the sounds of barking hounds. He would imagine it was the ghosts of Taton's men who were coming to hunt him down and kill him. He had an idea of how to make his way back up North but he didn't think he'd make it after so much time had passed. Who would help him find his son?

Finally, Big Bill decided it was time to leave the plantation and make an attempt at freedom before he died. He knew all the other slaves on the plantation had either died or had headed to freedom. So, it was time for him, too, to get away from there.

After traipsing through the dark swamp in circles, it seemed, he reached the mouth of a river and decided that here is where his life would end. He knew he could never find his way North by himself, with no guides from the

Underground Railroad. His wife was dead and if, by some miracle, he found his son, would his son even recognize him?

Big Bill felt hopeless and confused. As big as he was, he knew he'd never succeed at hiding and could easily be captured and sent back into slavery on some other plantation. That's how it always happened with runaways–if you weren't killed first. If, by some luck, you were returned to your master, you would be beaten into a bloody mess to teach you a lesson.

Big Bill had heard that big men like him were often used to breed stronger future slaves. He couldn't have that. His heart belonged to only one woman and since she was no longer with him, what purpose did he have to keep living?

Clutching his oversized axe to his chest Big Bill cannon bombed himself into the river, allowing himself to be welcomed into the bosom of Mother Water who, he hoped, would take his spirit back to his home, Africa, even though he didn't know his African name. He thought it was better to die by his own hand than to be stripped, whipped, humiliated, and beaten to death by white men.

Even in death, his spirit was set on finding Taton, avenging his wife's demise, and making Taton's spirit tell him his true African name. This is how Taton House had come to be haunted. Every night, Big Bill would roam the floors, dragging his heavy axe, moaning his sorrow. Big Bill's spirit would not rest until he was satisfied and, until then, Taton House would remain a haunted property.

CHAPTER SEVEN

He had tended to Taton House for nearly a generation. He had never seen the Taton House ghost himself, but he was told by his long dead aunties and uncles that night time was when Big Bill returned in search of Eugene Taton.

That night, when Big Bill returned to seek vengeance, he carried with him a heavy axe like the one used to murder his wife. Unfortunately, Taton had escaped through a back entrance (the one he used to use when he sneaked out into the slave cabins to steal their children) like the yellow-belly coward he was. Enraged, Big Bill had swung his axe wildly about, attacking anyone who stood in his path. Several of those killed were familiar faces, faces he remembered from the night of his wife's death. Many more died before Big Bill examined the bloody carnage: innocent house slaves who, Big Bill thought, were better off dead than living their lives in servitude; boarders who were white, others who heard the screams and came running, and those who had been sent by the cowardly Euguene Taton himself to catch him as he tried to escape to freedom with his family and the Underground Railroad guides.

Big Bill, the Taton House Ghost, could still be heard at night dragging his blood-stained ax as he continued to search for Old Man Taton, hell-bent on revenge.

This city girl don't stand a chance. Benjamin thought to himself. He tried to warn her, but she just paid him no mind. They all did that–thinking he wasn't in his right mind and then a clear moonless night'll come and *he'd* awaken, dragging that bloody ax of his and breathing heavy and moaning all at the same time. What they didn't know was that ole ghost wanted nothing to do with them.

Big Bill had his own agenda and wouldn't rest until his agenda had been met.

Benjamin would warn the many Taton House guests just to not get in the way of Big Bill when he went on his night searches. Just let him do what he was going to do. Don't turn on too many lights, either, because he hated that. It made him angry, as though you was preventing him from sneaking up on Ole Man Taton.

Benjamin thought about the new city chic who was now renting the house. She'd be ok just as long as she listened to Benjamin's advice, the words of wisdom that she so carelessly dismissed. He knew what would really make Big Bill leave...it was saying his African name. Benjamin knew what it was because his Auntie May had told him as a little boy. When he would sit at her knee on warm summer nights, she would tell him stories and her favorite one was the story of Big Bill, but the story always ended with a warning.

"Now, if'n you see his ghost and he's a comin' at yer," she would say, wagging a finger at him. "Don't yer go runnin' 'round. Jest say, 'Big Bill, yer African name is Kojo'." You see, Big Bill knew he was born in Ghana. He didn't know that in Ghana in those days, children were often named for the day of the week they was born on. Big Bill was born on a Monday and that is what his African name meant.

Benjamin tried to tell that city girl the same thing his Auntie Mae told him, but that city girl just gave him that dry smirk that people give when they think someone was crazy. Well, at least he told her. The rest was up to her. He hoped she listened to his advice.

CHAPTER EIGHT

Shemika couldn't wait to relax after her nice hot bath, complete with moisturizing bath oil to restore the life the southern heat had so mercilessly sucked from her. She padded down the winding staircase into the double parlour.

Plopping down on a stiff blue sofa, Shemika wrapped a throw blanket around her shoulders. The house was so chilly at night. The wooden floors seemed to be layered with ice. She decided that she'd unwind and read a book---she'd worry about story ideas later. If you wanted to write a good book, then you had to read a good book, she thought to herself.

Struggling to settle into the uncomfortable sofa cushions, her eyes caught sight of a portrait on the wall on the other side of the room. It was a framed oil painting of a bearded white man with angry, piercing dark eyes. He wore a broad brimmed gray hat that matched his drab grey suit. Walking over to the portrait in her bare feet, Shemika grazed a finger across the thickly layered painting.

Interesting, she thought to herself as her finger slid across the bumps and grooves of the dry oil paint. There was something unsettling about the man in the painting. Shemika imagined he was looking right back at her. Who was he and why would someone choose such a mean-looking and unattractive subject?

Leaning in close to the portrait, Shemika read the engraved brass label at the bottom. “Eugene Pavlov Taton”.

“Pavlov,” Shemika questioned aloud. “Ech!” She mocked, returning to the sofa and her book. Shemika knew that there was no way she’d be able to read with those eyes in that portrait looking at her. Each time she tried to read, she felt as though someone were watching her.

“Well, I guess I better try to write something,” she said aloud. She made her way up the winding staircase, each stair noisily creaking with her every step. She felt cold, although all but her feet were warmly covered.

Shemika slipped on a pair of socks she had packed. Grabbing her laptop from the Master Bedroom end table, she crept back downstairs to the parlour, aware of a change in the house’s atmosphere.

CHAPTER NINE

An hour had elapsed, and Shemeika hadn't written a darn thing outside of her outline. Occasionally glancing at the Taton portrait, she couldn't help but think the eyes of Old Man Taton were watching her. Giving in to lack of accomplishment, Shemika surfed the web and, perhaps, she'd be able to learn more about this creepy Old Man Taton.

"Dammit! No service?!!! How the hell am I supposed to work?!" she shouted, annoyed. Increasingly frustrated, Shemika slammed her laptop shut and picked up the book she had tried to read earlier. No sooner had she begun to read, fatigue overtook her.

Shemika didn't realize just how exhausted the heat of the day left her. Before she could read two pages of her book, her eyelids drooped in the dim light of the table lamp. Quickly, her body slumped into a sweet slumber. As the night encircled her in its cloak of darkness, an eerie silence permeated throughout Taton house.

A dim, thin sliver of light from the end table softly lay upon Shemika's body. As the night waned and the veil between the worlds grew increasingly thin, a heavy presence settled upon the house. The sound of the floorboards being scrapped as if something heavy were being dragged across it echoed above where Shemika lay.

Shemika frowned in her sleep but was not awakened. The sound continued. She tossed and turned on the sofa, the noise above her head disturbing her rest. Just as instantly as the sound came, it ceased and Shemika fell back into a deep slumber.

XXX

A sudden, ear-piercing, irritated moan filled the room where Shemika lay sprawled on the sofa. Startled, she bolted upright, her eyes wide with fear. The lamp next to the sofa exploded, the glass shattering, sprinkling her with its sharp shards. A burst of icy wind rushed against her face as though someone had suddenly swung open the front door during a blizzard. Shemika could see nothing but blackness.

A loud sound crashed against the wooden floorboards, followed by a splintering sound that traveled the length of the room. Rolling off the sofa, Shemika stumbled in the room's ebonyness in search of one of the very few recently added light switches. Finding a wall, she desperately crawled her fingers across the chilly walls. She peered into the darkness as the dragging sound grew louder. She could feel the noise moving towards her and she panicked.

"Who-who's there?" she asked the darkness. All she received in response was a moaning sound. Sweat dampened her forehead despite the chilliness of the room.

"Identify yourself!" she screamed. More moaning and dragging. Suddenly, the noise was fast upon her. In her fear, Shemika unknowingly slammed her back against the portrait of Old Man Taton. She slid down to her knees and sobbed.

"Please, please, don't hurt me," she whimpered, covering her face with her hands and bracing for whatever deadly fate awaited her.

The moaning and dragging sound increased until it was no longer bearable. Screaming, Shemika covered her ears as the weight of the chaos fell upon her body. The entire house shook tremendously, as though it would rattle from its very foundation and, almost instantly, there was silence. The only audible sound was the chiming of the parlor's grandfather clock.

CHAPTER TEN

In the eerie silence, chilly hands slithered over Shemika's shoulders and she released a blood-curdling scream. In desperation, she tried to shake her shoulder free from the invisible bone-chilling hands that refused to release her.

"Let me go!" she screamed. Suddenly, she felt a storm-like blast of frigid air blast into her body, propelling her back against the wall.

"LEAVE HER ALOOOOOONE!" a voice yelled, quaking the entire house. In the darkness, she noticed a glint of something perhaps made of metal. With instant fear paralyzing her, her eyes widened as the blade of an ax came crashing down towards her. She ducked her head in between her knees as she sat in a fetal position on the floor. With what she believed was her last breath, she screamed and prepared herself for her deadly fate. She suddenly remembered what Benjamin had told her when she was loading her bags into the house. She initially thought the old man was missing a few marbles but right now, she had nothing to lose but her life, which was already in question.

"KOJO!" she shouted with feigned authority. "Your African name, Big Bill, is Kojo!" Silence. The entire room seemed to pause. Shemika looked up into the darkness, trembling. She heard a long, drawn-out sigh.

"AAAAAAAAAAHHHHHHHHHH, thannnnnnk yoooooooou!" a deep, masculine voice boomed inside the room. The frigid air suddenly seemed to be sucked out of the room and Shemika grabbed on to a nearby display cabinet in order to prevent herself from being taken with the air. She heard a door slam, and the house was still.

She could hear the old grandfather clock announce midnight.

CHAPTER ELEVEN

She was alive.

Dawn swept through the dusty curtains.With a tear-streaked face, she squinted into the beams of sunlight that had somehow crept into the room. Rising to her feet, she turned to notice that the portrait of Old Man Taton remained attached to its place on the wall, yet it had been slashed down the middle and what oozed from it was a sticky substance not unlike that of blood. Not waiting for anything else to happen, Shemika rushed to gather her things and get the hell out of that house!

Outside, birds chirped in the morning sun. The grass, kissed by sweet dew, bent as rabbits playfully and innocently frolicked across the fields. Benjamin Cummings, humming to himself, drove past the house in his tractor as he did every morning. Today, he seemed to smile as he passed Taton House, the old house that held old secrets. The Old House, where Big Bill finally got his vengeance.

The House on Maple Ave.

We used to walk by every day after school. The windows were always dark, and the lawn was overgrown with grass and weeds. The grownups said that no one lived in that old decrypt house because it was so unkempt, but one day my friends and I were coming home from the neighborhood playground and saw otherwise.

There, amidst the overgrowth of the front lawn, stood a girl about our age. Her face was gray like ash and her hair hung in limp strands about her head. She wore a plaid jumper skirt, a dingy white, long-sleeved blouse. Her eyes were wide and expressionless. We stopped on our bikes and waved at her.

“Hey, how’re you doing? Do you live there? Are you new here?” She continued to look at us with wide, vacant eyes that were encircled with blackness. Her lips did not move, she said nothing.

“Well, I’m John and this is Paul, and that’s Jared. We live in the neighborhood. Wanna go with us to the playground some time? You can borrow my bike if you don’t have one.” I said. Still no response.

“Okay, see you ‘round.” We rode our bikes away, and the girl slowly turned her head in our departing direction.

Later that afternoon, as my friends and I were talking on the playground about the strange girl, Jared said that his old sister once told him a story about a girl who died in that house a long time ago.

“And they said she just died,” Jared's conspiratory whispered. “She just died in the house! She was really sick and her skin was pale and back then they didn’t have medicines and stuff so she just died. I don’t know where she’s buried, but my sister says her spirit sometimes shows up at that creepy ole house on Maple and just stands there.

“So you’re saying we saw a ghost and not a real live girl?” I asked.

“I’m just sayin’ what my sister said.” Jared answered, lowering his eyes.

The next day, we went to Maple Ave again to see if the girl was standing outside the house. I didn’t believe in ghosts, but Jared was sold. I wasn’t sure about Paul,though whose face wore no expression.

I intended to go right into the yard. We saw her. She was standing in the same place. This time, she was sitting on an old rickety swing that was tied to a tree in the front yard. She didn't speak when I waved.

"Hi", I said. She just stared at me with glassy eyes. The other boys tried to tell me not to go inside the yard. I opened the gate, its rickety squeak alerting the girl of my presence. The girl stopped swinging and turned towards me. She stared at me as I got closer to her.

"Hey you wanna come with us to the playground?" She said nothing. I touched her shoulder and quickly withdrew my hand in shock. She was ice cold despite her clothing.

"Well, if you wanna sometime, you could come join us," I said. I backed out of the yard, feeling goosebumps suddenly covering my entire body.

When we were at the playground with our bikes, I told the boys how cold the girl felt when I touched her.

Jared said, "Told ya! She ain't not among the living," he added with a mysteriously sounding whisper in my face. I pushed him away.

"So you're saying I touched a ghost?" I said with increasingly vanishing disbelief.

"You touched a dead person!" Jared said.

Pete said, "You know you should just stop going by there and talking to her. She obviously ain't interested, and *then* you went and *touched* her!"

That night, as I slept, I tossed and turned. I couldn't get that girl's face out of my mind. It was like she was haunting my brain!

My window blew open, blanketing my bedroom in the cool night air. I sat up in bed and made a move to shut the window, but hesitated. Suddenly, there was the girl standing at the foot of my bed, looking at me with those expressionless eyes. Both startled and frightened, I scrunched up against my headboard.

"What do you want?" I whimpered, bed sheets up to my chin.

"Your soooooullllll," the girl said, her mouth an endless black hole.

At least she finally talked, I thought. She stretched out a hand towards me and seemed to float in the air right where she was standing.

"I want your soooooouuuuul," she said, again. I yelled for my parents, but no one came.

"It's been a looooong time since I have eaten. I am huuuuuunnnnngry," she said.

"If you're hungry," I shouted in defiance." There are some cookies downstairs!"

"I don't need that food. I need your soooooouuuuul!"

"Why do you need my soul?" The girl laughed and her laugh echoed throughout my room. I screamed. Instantly, there was the sound of footsteps coming up the stairs. My door smashed open and my parents were standing next to my bed.

"Are you all right, John?" my mom asked, wrapping her arms around me. I pointed to the foot of my bed, but the girl was no longer there.

"She *was* there!" I cried, burying my head into my mother's mom.

"Who?" my dad said.

"The girl at the house on Maple Ave!" My parents looked at each other knowingly. They knew something they weren't telling me. My mother walked over to the window and closed it.

"John, you need to stop going by that house," my mom said, a serious look on her face." A girl died in that and her spirit lives there. She tries to come back to the world of the living and anyone she catches, she takes their soul so she can live again. Stay away from that house."

"But Mom, I touched her, and she felt real!"

"You *touched* her?" My mother's eyes were suddenly wide with astonishment.

"I just touched her shoulder, and she was cold."

"You touched her," my father said. "Now she's going to keep coming back for your soul. We have to stop her. We have to make sure her ghost is gone for good." My mother nodded in agreement.

"John, I want you to do something and we must do it tonight while the moon is still full," my mother said.

My parents took me to the attic. I've never been in the attic. My father pulled out a big heavy box, opened it. My mother pulled a mason jar from the box while my father grabbed two seven-day candles: one red and one white.

They led me to the kitchen where my mother poured the thick red muddy-looking liquid from the mason jar into a tall glass of milk that she warmed in the microwave.

"Drink this—" she held out the glass to me.

"Um, mom—-"

"*All* of it." she said, firmly. I drank.

"Yuck, what is this?"

"She will return every night until she gains your soul. This will mix with your blood so that when she reaches inside your body for your soul, she will be poisoned."

"The milk is for you, to keep you in a sleepy state," my father added.

"What's in this stuff?" I asked, again.

"That is not important. You just finish all of it." So I did.

"You will soon feel tired," my mom said. "That is to trick her into thinking you are an easy target and that taking your soul will be easy.

"The red candles represent blood and are to draw her in. The white candle is to banish her from our world by summoning and attracting the gatekeeper spirits who will take her back to her soul where it resides in the world of the undead where she can no longer bypass the light and enter our world to feed off the souls of the living.

"How do you know all of this?" I asked.

"Your mother and I were kids once, too, in this town. That girl was deathly sick and died in that house when you grandma was a kid," my father answered.

As my eyelids drooped, my mother explained that after my Mima got married, she gave birth to my mother and later my aunts and uncles , she made a jar of that stuff because people spoke of the girl returning. Kids were suddenly disappearing and my Mima knew she had to teach her children how to make the liquid and always keep it in a mason jar in a nice, dry place in their homes.

"Appalachian magick," my mom called it. My Mima was a witch who practiced a lot of Appalachian magick before she moved here to the valley after her husband, my Papi, transitioned. She said that she was getting too old for the mountains.

For the rest of the night, sleep wasn't as restless as I thought it would be. I went back to bed knowing that something was going to happen that night. Would she return on the same night? I guess she would keep coming until she got my soul, no matter how many tries that took her.

Although I dozed off and on in my bed, I could not fall completely asleep. I stared at the two lit candles my father had placed at my bedside. The house was so eerily quiet. My parents had said that they would camp outside my bedroom door just in case things didn't go well. They had blankets and pillows strewn in the hallway outside my bedroom, and I could hear my father's loud snoring. I really didn't want to see the girl again. I was afraid. Unfortunately, my eyes slowly closed in slumber.

"Heeeelllleeennn!" a scratchy voice awakened me.

"My name is Heelleenn!" It was the girl floating at the foot of my bed, her eyes now as dark and round as her abysmal mouth.

"Tonight, I will have your sooooouuuuuullllllll!" I shivered and braced for the impact of her hand being thrust through my chest. Frozen with fear, I sat up in bed.

"Then, come get it, Helen!" I said between clenched teeth, feigning bravery. My words seemed to anger her and she let out an ear-piercing scream. She waved an arm towards my bedroom door and I heard it lock. I could hear my parents banging on the door and jiggling the handle to no avail. I was trapped inside of my bedroom with Helen, who wanted my soul. My only consolation was knowing she'd be poisoned as soon as she reached into my body–at least, I hoped she would.

Helen flew towards me, an icy wind trailing behind her like the train of a wedding gown. She screamed again in my face, her frigid breath smelling of death and decay. I turned my head in disgust as a pain shot through my chest. She had shoved her hand into the depths of my body in order to retrieve my soul, which she so desperately wanted.. When she withdrew her arm, her once dingy white sleeve was covered in blood–my blood. Again, she reached into my chest, this time screaming as though she had been stabbed. She looked at me in utter disgust. Astonishment and fear colored her ghoulish face. A line of red liquid rushed up her boney fingers, arms and neck. Her hollow eyes narrowed.

"You tricckked meeeee, you bad, bad boy!" she screamed into my face. Just as she drew back her arm, exposing sharp claws, another blast of wind blew open my bedroom window. With blurred vision, I could make out the appearance of several figures bathed in blinding white robes ascending upon the girl who had now become so agitated that she growled and clawed at my bedpost. She was being grabbed and dragged away from my bed towards the open window. She emitted the most unearthly sounds until finally, the air was sucked out of my room, closing the window and popping open my bedroom door. My parents fell into the room crying and throwing their arms around me. Before I closed my eyes from sheer exhaustion, I saw the white candle go out, followed by an unnoticed shattering of the candle in the red glass jar. Millions of glass shards remained on my bureau.

Helen was gone, and I was safe.

UNGRATEFUL

"Twenty-two... twenty-three... twenty-four... twenty-five…" Fifteen more squats and Dorsey would be finished with her morning workout. She got up every day at four a.m. to prepare for the day ahead. However, despite her best efforts Dorsey could never obtain the physique of the celebrity women of color she saw in *Ebony Magazine*. She was too curvy. Her hips, although perfect for bearing children, were far too broad. Her thighs would never be skinny and her bosom would never shrink. Her only saving grace was her enviably smooth tummy, and the result was her hourglass shape.

That shape is what attracted him to her. They were both young and seemingly in love, although it would later become clear that he was more in lust than in love. Back then, he couldn't keep his hands off her. They had three children together: Justin, now nineteen, Ethan, age ten and little Soozie just seven years old. Beyond the passion of those early days, he became restless and unsatisfied. Vulnerable to the temptation of "other beauties," when confronted he rationalized his infidelity by claiming that he could not be limited to having "just one woman." Dorsey, tired of his nonsense, filed for divorce. Surprisingly, he put up no fight. He gave her whatever she wanted, just so long as he was able to keep doing what *he* wanted.

What *he* wanted included sleeping over her apartment anytime, unannounced. He claimed he was, "seeing the kids." He paid his obligations and Dorsey never wanted for anything during the now four years of divorce, except that she longed to be loved again--truly loved--by a man. She wanted to feel beautiful, desirable even. She wanted to have a man who loved her, and only her, the way she had once loved him, before it became clear that he did not have the character necessary to reciprocate.

"What'ya got up in here for a grown man to eat?" he asked, interrupting her morning routine. "Cereal and toast won't cut it." He yawned, scratching his increasingly round belly. She didn't answer as his presence disgusted her. Laughing, he wrapped his arms around her waist, letting his elbow rest on her broad hips. He attempted to kiss her and she pushed him away, annoyed.

"You know I still love you but I need *more* , baby." He was a constant irritation, but helpful when she needed him to be. He would make sure the kids were up, fed, and ready for school while she bustled around the apartment trying to get herself ready for another day of work.

Dorsey taught Criminal Justice Studies at City College, but it was two hours away and, after seeing her own children off to school, she'd drive her sometimes reliable car to the Park 'n Ride where she awaited the bus that would take her to work. Back in the day, she had hoped of becoming a criminal attorney, but then she met Tyrone and soon after she had Justin. Although she didn't drop out of school, she did have to put aside her aspirations to take care of the kids while Tyrone finished his degree and later, when he opened his own consulting business where he was able to land high paying and desperate firms eager to get a leg up in the world. The money he didn't blow on booze and women, he used to take care of Dorsey and the kids and pay back his small business loan. When it came to work, Tyrone was a serious, level-headed, savvy businessman but, when it came to commitment, he was a careless juvenile.

How Dorsey longed to be young and attractive again! To feel a man's eyes approvingly traveling over her body, a body that she no longer had. If she could just start all over again, erase Tyrone, their children, her out-of-shape body. She wouldn't make the mistake of another Tyrone again! She wouldn't get tied down. She'd keep all her "goods" to herself and tease the men until she felt like one was deserving of her body. She'd do just what Tyrone did: love 'em and leave 'em. She was done with being tossed aside. She'd be the one calling the shots and no one was getting a piece of her pie without her consent. They would experience the desire to be loved as she had desired to be loved. They would feel the pain of dissatisfaction just like she had felt that pain. It would be her turn to be on top, figuratively and literally, and only when, only if and when, she wanted.

After Tyrone and the kids had gone, Dorsey sat in her car at the Park 'n Ride unsure of whether she wanted to head into work at all. What did it matter anyway? No one ever cared about her at work. Her students were unmotivated, her colleagues jaded. She fingered a bottle in her purse, a secret purchase she had made last weekend on her way home from work. The shop was only open during the evenings and late nights, and it just so happened that Dorsey had a late class that evening. She told the kids she'd be home late and had already had supper in the refrigerator for her oldest to warm in the microwave. He was responsible enough. He'd make sure his siblings finished their homework, took showers, brushed their teeth, said their prayers, and went to bed on time. He was good like that.

Dorsey pulled the vial from her purse, popping the cork on top of the fruity red-colored liquid that swirled around in the glass. She downed the sour-tasting fluid. The vial fell to the floor as Dorsey bent over from the pain exploding in her abdomen. Sweat beaded her forehead and trickled down her arms. Her legs contorted, stretched and then shrank back to reveal toned muscles. Struggling to breathe, Dorsey opened the door to her car and fell to the ground in pain. The world whirled around her in a twisted, writhing rainbow of colors before the blackness covered her vision.

Purple heels clicked on the concrete as she sashayed down the sidewalk. Her hips parted the crowd like Moses parting the Red Sea. She sported a purple broad-brimmed hat and a matching pocketbook that bumped her side as she walked. Her body was adorned in a daffodil yellow and lavender dress that swooped below her neck, exposing her abundant cleavage. Her dress cinched at her waist and flared out at the knees. An orchestra of leering whistles followed her as she held her chin up high and pointed her nose towards the sun. She was FAB and no one could tell her otherwise. No man owned her heart and no kid begged for her attention. She was just as free as she wanted to be, and she wanted to be as free as she could.

She arrived at her multi-level condo, kicked off her designer heels, tossed her keys and purse on the kitchen counter, and hummed happily as she pulled a bottle of Dom Perignon from her wine fridge and poured herself a glass.

"To me!" she chuckled, toasting herself. Her cellphone rang. Annoyed, she looked at it and wrinkled her nose. *Another wannabe lover. Let them chase.* She'd not be a slave to any man ever again.

"This is *my* time," she said out loud and poured herself another glass which she instantly downed followed by another and another until the bottle was empty. Why not? She could do whatever she wanted.

"You look well, Dorsey" came a voice from behind her. Startled, she whirled around to face the voice. A small, plump woman emerged from the shadows of the adjoining room.

"Thanks to you and your mojo," replied Dorsey, as she stumbled towards the woman who remained silent, wrinkled hands clasped together in front of her. Despite her age, her silvery hair hung in vibrant shiny curls that kissed her rounded shoulders.

"Everything is as you like it?" the old woman inquired. Dorsey looked up as if nothing in her life could be better than it was at that very moment.

"All is perfect." Their eyes met as the old woman nodded.

"I have come to collect," she said.

"Collect? Oh yes, I'll get that to you soon, " Dorsey said, dismissing the old woman with a wave of her hand.

"You have said that before, twice, and I have been generous in my understanding, but the time to pay... is now."

"Old woman," Dorsey stood, towering, staggering, and wagging a finger into her face, "I have the perfect life now. Everything I ever wanted: attention, money, freedom, beauty for days, and nothing but time. When I say I'll pay you your due, I mean *I'll pay you your due!* Just not right now."

"It is not wise to leave a debt, child," the old woman replied.

"It is not wise to leave a debt, "Dorsey mimicked, scrunching up her face. "I'm done talking to you, old woman! Get out of my-----"

"You will---"

"GET OUT NOW!" Dorsey screamed, gripping the old woman's fragile arm and pushing her out the front door of her apartment.

Before Dorsey could close the door, the old woman turned and spoke, "You will regret not honoring your debt."

"Whatever, old bag!" Dorsey shouted, slamming the door on the old woman.

The sun was high in the blue canvas sky, and music blared from a red convertible as it cruised down the highway.

Ain't no stopping us now! Nope. No one would ever again cause her to feel inferior. She was on top of the world and was not looking back. She was free, free of *him,* free of all of them. She was sexy, too. She was the one who was desired, and she would make them beg, long, and wish, just like she used to do when she was ugly. Yep. Now she'd be the one in control. From now on, she would take what she wanted, and the only thing she wanted was her newfound power. So what, an old witch had helped her get it? No one had to know, and she wasn't about to tell. As far as she was concerned, that old woman was a hoodoo, voodoo, nobody who worked a good spell but--she hadn't really thrown that old woman out of her place two nights ago, did she? Did that woman really appear in her apartment? Naaa---just a bad dream combined with too much alcohol. She really had to ease up on the booze, but not right now. She'd get that old woman her pay, but when she felt like it. She had already given her the blood of *him* and *them.* She had laced their food with the powder so they'd fall into a deep sleep, and while they were out Dorsey had pricked them and caught the blood. What the old woman wanted was for Dorsey to fill the vial with the blood of the men she slept with. Well, Dorsey had forgotten the last three times, and the old woman bought all of Dorsey's excuses, but the old woman seemed a little upset now.

Dorsey pulled into the parking garage of the mall set on spending some quality time at Fit Shoes & Fancy. She sure needed some heels to match the new cocktail dress she would be wearing to the company dinner with the other executives from her new job as the President of Design and Marketing. No longer would she be stuck with college students who didn't want to learn and colleagues resigned to lives that were mundane and seemingly not worth the effort. With her eye for color and style, her career now put her at the front lines of the industry.

That ol' bag came through on her word. Even if it were really Dorsey who did all the heavy lifting. Imagine poisoning all those lovers, and Tyrone. Besides the child support he provided, he hadn't been any use to her in years. And he still thought he was gonna get some after all his cheating? Um… no.

Her platform sandals clopped on the floor of the parking garage, echoing off its empty floor, walls, and low ceiling. For noon on a Saturday, it was odd for the mall to be so vacant. Nevertheless, matching shoes couldn't wait and Friday would be here before you knew it. Dorsey boarded the elevator, gaudy pocketbook hanging from her arm. She pressed the main level button, humming to the elevator's nineties pop music. The door opened onto a mall store strangely devoid of the normal human shuffle. Dorsey noticed that she was alone in the mall, but dismissed it.

There must be some big event in town holding everybody up. Dorsey reassured herself. *Surely, these floors will be packed soon. At least, I'll be first in line to get my shoes on sale!*

With a shiver, Dorsey noticed that it was unusually chilly in the mall as if the air conditioners had run all night long though it wasn't even hot enough outside. The emptiness began to make Dorsey nervous, so she sped up her pace toward Fit Shoes & Fancy at the end of the promenade.

"Good morning and welcome," smiled a cashier in a pretty-yet-dusty- pink blouse and white skirt. Her jet black hair hung like old curtains about her head. Dorsey noticed with some disgust that the young woman's teeth were brown-stained and that a few were missing.

Managers must be desperate. Dorsey thought. Again, Dorsey observed that she was the only shopper present yet she assumed that this would work to her advantage. Heading over to the dress shoes, Dorsey decided to slow down. There'd be no rush today. She could do what she wanted, how she wanted, and take her own sweet time, too, if she felt like it. A pair of silver stilettos caught her attention. Dorsey's eyes grew wide like a hungry cat as she noticed that the heels were encrusted with a glitter of crushed diamonds. They were the only pair of shoes like that in the store, in the world perhaps, she thought as she turned one of the fabulously glitter shoes over and over in her hands.

Just my size! How fortunate! She would wear these beauties out of the store as they were too beautiful to be carried in a bag.

Whipping out her credit card at the counter, Dorsey averted her eyes from the cashier's rotten teeth. She stifled a grimace as a pungent odor emanated, seemingly, from the woman herself. It sickened Dorothy's stomach. It smelled like meat, turned from being left unrefrigerated or, to be exact, like decaying human flesh.

"I won't be needing a box and you can toss these old sandals. I'm going to wear these babies right now." The cashier nodded, looking Dorsey right in the eyes, causing her blood to run cold.

"Take care and do be careful, ma'am," was all the cashier said when

Dorsey smoothed her yellow and white striped knee-length sundress.

Odd.

Spirits high, Dorsey strutted out of the store and down the main level floor towards the parking garage elevators.

"Nice shoes, ma'am," came a voice from behind. Dorsey laughed pretentiously and waved a "thank you" without looking back. Suddenly, she felt as though she were surrounded by admirers although she couldn't make out any of their faces.

Must be the glare of the sunlight coming in from the mall glass ceilings, she thought.

"Oooooh, don't she look sharp!" came another voice. When Dorsey turned towards the voice, all she saw was a blur of crowded bodies lining the halls. She slowly blinked her eyes in an attempt to clear her vision yet there was still a blur.

Must be low sugar, she thought, although it'd been years since she experienced her vision blur due to low sugar.

"Those must have been expensive, " a woman's voice said to her. Dorsey's head began to spin and she became very unsteady on her new dressed up feet.

"She's so fancy!"

"She's so sophisticated!"

"High class!"

"Diamonds on the soles of her shoes!" the voices came from every direction and Dorsey found herself unable to walk any further. She held her cloudy head in one hand and attempted to steady herself by pressing her knees together.

There was that smell again. The smell that invaded her nose when she paid for her shoes. The smell from that cashier. It made her stomach turn. She felt as though she were going to vomit.

Perspiration grew on Dorsey's forehead and spilled down her temples.

"Help." she whimpered, teetering on her heels. The voices, now indecipherable, continued to whirl around her in a nightmarish haze of gibberish.

"Please. My eyes. Someone help." she stammered, reaching out the hand that once held her head to the crowd of blur.

"Aw, Miss Fancy shoes don't feel well," came a craggy voice, causing Dorsey to draw back, insulted.

"I guess those shoes weren't worth all the trouble, now were they, Dorsey" came another mean and insulting voice.

"Who said that? " Dorsey blindly whirled around in search of the insulting faces whose mouths poured forth such hate but all she could see was a messy mixture of blurred colors.

"Maybe then you could help me. I-I need medical assistance--"

"Oh, you want *more* help, now, do you?"

"We've all seen just how *grateful* you were when we helped you before, right?"

"Please, I-I don't know what you're talking about." Dorsey helplessly sank to her knees, still trying to locate the owners of the ugly voices.

"How are you at paying your debts, *Dorsey?*"

"Please, I don't feel well! I need help."

"No one wants to help *ungratefuls* like you, Dorsey." The voices seemed to be closing in on her. The blur of the crowd was closer and surrounded her on all sides.

"Please, no--"

"When you don't pay your debt, *Dorsey*, we come to collect."

"Please--I'm sorry! I didn't mean to rip off the old lady, I--"

"It's too late. Your bill is past due."

"No--"

"Too late, *Dorsey*. Time to collect." Dorsey felt her throat clench from the vile stench of death that gradually began to suffocate her. With each passing second, her heart rate began to increase, causing her to become nauseous, and she vomited all over herself. The combined smell of death and her own vomit repulsed her. She was slick with sweat. Unable to help herself, she submitted to the approaching darkness as the figures around her mixed together, creating a blanket of black that both surrounded and engulfed her and the thumping in her chest ceased to be.

A body was found Saturday morning just as the mall stores were opening. The approximate time of death was midnight on Friday. A pool of blood flowed from under the woman's head. There were no signs of a struggle and the authorities wonder how this unidentified woman seemingly got into the mall after closing and now lay there dead on the mall floor. They figured that she could have already been somewhere inside the mall when it closed. There were no cars in the parking garage. The woman was a mess. Her hair was dishevelled. Her clothes were plain and worn, and her fingernails were cracked and dirty. The officers at the scene noted that she had no identification in her purse although one officer thought he recognized her.

" Jess, come over here! This woman looks like my old college professor, the one who taught Criminal Justice," the officer said to his colleague.

"You mean the Black lady?"

"Yeah, her." He said, as he shook his head, looking at the sad sight of what was obviously a tragedy.

"Word had it that she went missing. Guess we know what she's been up to," she said, implying that her last job may have been less vertical than the one at the college.

"Jess, that ain't kind. She always reminded me of my mama."

"Oh, Randall, I didn't know you had a crush ---"

"That ain't funny!" Randall couldn't believe his partner was joking about this woman who had obviously fallen on hard times. The two gazed down in silence at the lifeless body. After what seemed like an eternity, Randall broke the silence.

“I wonder what happened to her to land her here like this and in this condition.”

“Who cares? She’s dead.” Randall had had enough of his partner’s insensitivities and decided it was time to call in the morgue unit to remove the body.

“Let’s get a move on.The coroner should be here soon.” As both officers turned away from the body, Jess took one last look at the body and noticed something strange.

“Are those stilettos with fake diamonds,” she grimaced at the shabby grey shoes on the poor woman’s swollen feet. “Gosh, those have to be the ugliest shoes I’ve ever seen.”

UNFORGIVEN

What happens to a dream deferred?
Does it dry up
Like a raisin in the sun?
Or fester like a sore--
And then run?
Does it stink like rotten meat?
Or crust and sugar over--
Like a syrupy sweet?
Maybe it just sags
Like a heavy load.
Or does it explode?

-Langston Hughes, "Harlem"

What a dreary day, he thought to himself as he shrugged off his wet boots and coat. His damp brown skin dripped from the sudden summer rain. Happy to be home, he smiled as his fat orange cat rubbed against his leg.

"Tabitha," he said, hefting the cat's heavy body and cradling her in his arms. "You've got to go on a diet."

He decided he'd amuse himself with some television before dragging himself into the kitchen to make yet another sad microwave meal. No worries. At least there won't be any dishes to clean, he thought to himself as he slumped down into his overstuffed easy chair, orange tabby on his lap, relieved to be in his nice, dry apartment.

Very well indeed, he smiled smugly. Very well indeed. She used to say that. She, now gone but always present. She, whose voice echoed through his mind, invading his thoughts on an almost daily basis. She, whose picture stood out from the wall, like a traffic signal, warning him at every moment of every day.

He glanced over to her picture on the mantel, and she stared back at him from above the fireplace. Her Black face was creased with line upon line, each one of them a testimony to her long sad life. Her white hair, neatly curled about her head, accentuated the stern look in her eyes as she glared at him from her chair.

She didn't always look like that. Once she was soft and beautiful and her eyes would sparkle like diamonds with the vitality and excitement of youth. How he loved her so! Her cherry blossom lips would call to him during their rendezvous beneath the apple tree on his father's farm.

He had courted her - that's what young men did back in those days - for nearly a year before he had asked for her hand. She was so beautiful, and he dreamed of running away with her far, far away from the backbreaking work on his father's farm. He was going to make his fortune in the big cities up North. He'd get a real job while she would tend to the children and the house - the house he hoped to buy with the money he was going to make. That's what successful Black families did back in his day.

But married life and the big city life weren't all either of them had imagined. It wasn't easy for a Black man from the South to get a job with decent pay. He tried and tried but it was never enough. And the children - they had dreamed of a large family - but they only managed to produce one child - a boy, Trevor, named after her brother who had been good to them back home.

She grew more unhappy with each failed attempt to conceive another child. The apartment was cold and small, and she longed for the warmth and space of the South. She knew he could find work back home, and she begged him to leave. She thought that one day he could take over his father's farm, but he refused, saying he didn't want to crawl back like a broken and a failed man. Over time, she gave up trying and became more and more despondent. She hardly spoke to him when he came home, except to tell him that his meal was "on the stove."

Her once bright eyes shone not at all and her growing unhappiness produced the growing lines on her face when it happened.

The streets were filled with kids during the summer. They played basketball using hoops made from milk crates. No one had to know anyone. They only had to know how to play. Back in his time, Black boys judged one another by the game, not by the green in their pockets because, after all, hardly anyone had any money.

Their son was exceptional. One day, she knew, he would become a star, and they'd move away from the dingy, overcrowded streets. She was so proud of Trevor. They'd finally be free and sometimes, it looked as if her eyes hinted at the possibilities of happiness.

Trevor had grown into a tall, muscular and handsome young man. One hot and humid summer night, he was walking back home from a scrimmage basketball game, a towel thrown over his damp, sweaty shoulders. Now that he was old enough, he could walk by himself to the neighborhood court, no more playing in the street with a milk crate for a hoop for him. Someday, he was going to be a professional and earn lots of money to buy his mom and dad a nice big home in a nice place far away from this nasty city.

She warned him not to stay out too late. The streets were not safe at night for Black boys, especially ones who walked alone.

“No good can come out of you being stubborn like your father,” she had said that night. But now it was late and she paced the kitchen floor, worry creasing her forehead. Hours passed and no heavy and familiar footsteps ascended the rickety stairs.

He didn’t suffer long. He never saw it coming. They were five, and they were fast. Of course they were, those cowards never traveled alone, alone like Trevor was the night it happened.

They jumped Trevor from behind and one of them stabbed Trevor with a knife. He was found the next morning by a family on their way to church, little girls dressed for Sunday school. Trevor's body lay on the sidewalk, his blood pooled from where he had bled out alone in the night.

The assailants were never found as no one really bothered to look.

She blamed him for Trevor's death. He knew that. If they had moved back down South, if they had lived on his father's farm, Trevor would still be alive. There would have been loads of strong Black cousins who would be around to look after Trevor, and he would never have to be alone. He had said that the opportunities and the education were better up here, but what did any of that matter now?

Sadness turned to sorrow. She no longer cared what she looked like. The apartment accumulated dust. She lost her soul the night Trevor was killed and her eyes reflected nothing but emptiness every time she looked at him. When he came home from work, his meals were no longer "on the stove." They occupied the same space, but they no longer lived, together or otherwise.

It went on like that for days which turned into weeks, which turned into months, which turned into years.

People said that it was that sadness that ultimately killed her. Others said that her spirit had become consumed, first with living a loveless life and the desire to return to the South, then by the loss of her only hope. When Trevor died, she died, too.

He never moved from the apartment. Everything remained as it had always been. Now that it was only he and the orange tabby who occupied the cramped dusty space, he could come and go as he pleased. He worked to pay the bills. He worked to keep busy.

Sitting across from her picture, stroking his tabby, the dim light reflecting his silver hair, he thought to himself how she was never really happy here and that she had always blamed him for her unhappiness.

Her frozen portrait glared down its final judgment. Tabitha mewed.

Why did you leave the farm? He heard her ask. Trevor is dead because of you. He heard her say.

"I only tried to make life better for us," he said aloud.

You were always stubborn.

"I loved you so much. Remember, when we were young--"

That was a long time ago.

"You were happy then."

Because we didn't live here.

"Did you ever love me?"

Why do you ask me that?

"We had big dreams."

You ruined everything!

"We were going to raise a family in a house of our own."

We had nothing. We were never going to have anything. Your dreams were a waste of time. Your stubbornness killed our son!

He stood, Tabitha plopping to the worn carpet. He slowly approached her picture.

"I tried my best."

Stupid.

"Please, forgive me."

No response.

"Forgive me. I miss you terribly." Her eyes grew darker and he fell to the floor in despair. He reached out his hand only to be shunned.

All you had to do was take us back to the farm and our son would still be alive. You killed Trevor! You killed me!

"No, I tried to --"

Now, you shall perish in this box you call a home and you shall perish alone.

No one will mourn you. No one will care. No one will even know.

"Baby, I only wanted to give you the best."

Silence.

Thirty days passed. Only when a foul stench permeated the hallway did anyone think to check on the old man who lived on the second floor. Finally, the landlord showed up and forced the door open.

The smell was horrible. Dust layered the shelves and the furniture. The air itself was rotten. Roaches scuttled away from the light. The landlord discovered the corpse, wrinkled and decayed. He was sprawled on his backside, a picture frame clutched to his chest. The old man must have fallen after taking the picture from the wall, the landlord thought.

The landlord looked at the picture. The smiling faces of a young and attractive brown skinned couple with a little boy who looked up at them with unconditional love in his eyes. The three of them were frozen in time striding down what appeared to be a long dirt road.

Captive Song

There once was an old woman who lived in a tiny hut at the edge of a village. The villagers had long ago stopped wondering why this woman had chosen to live apart from everyone else. She had no children and no husband. She spent her days sweeping her home with a whisk broom and tending to her small garden. Early mornings, she would go for walks in the forest to gather flowers and herbs from which she made medicines.

Despite her lack of human companionship, the old woman was very happy with her life. No one bothered her and she bothered no one.

It was during one of these morning walks that the old woman happened upon a small bird lying in the mud and the leaves of the forest floor. The helpless little bird chirped desperately as he struggled to flap his muddy wings.

“Oh, dear bird, I will take you home and care for you,” the woman said as she gently scooped up the wounded little bird and carried him back to her hut.

Back in her hut, the woman bathed the little bird in a basin filled with warm water and sweet herbs. As she washed off the mud, the woman gasped. The bird’s feathers, which had been scrunched up and caked with mud, now unfurled to reveal all the colors of the rainbow. His tail fanned out and hung from his backside like a shimmering waterfall. Finally, he opened his beautiful, brilliantly-colored wings and stood proudly.

“I shall name you Dadou,” the woman announced, kissing the beautiful bird.

In the days and weeks to follow, Dadou grew stronger and would accompany the woman on her walks.

The bird would sing such enchanting songs that all of the forest's creatures were mesmerized. Dadou's melodies floated on the wind down into the village where all the villagers smiled and hummed as they went about their day enjoying the magical sound of the old woman's special friend.

Soon everyone, humans and animals alike, looked forward to the music as they began each day.

The old woman grew very fond of Dadou and knew that as he grew stronger he would want to return to his proper home. How the woman dreaded the thought releasing him. What would her life be like without the happy and melodious sounds that she had come to rely upon?

Eager to prevent the bird from leaving, the old woman stopped taking

Dadou on her early morning walks through the forest.

"You need to rest your wings," she'd tell him. Dadou grew increasingly sad because he longed to be with the woman and so he would sing sad songs when she was away. In time, all the villagers and the animals of the forest could also hear the little bird's soulful lamenting and they, too, became sad.

When the woman returned from her walk one day she made Dadou's favorite soup with the fresh ingredients from her garden, but Dadou wasn't hungry. In fact, Dadou refused to eat even one bite.

"Dadou, why don't you eat?" The bird turned his beautiful tail feathers towards the woman and hung his head in sorrow.

"If you don't eat, you won't get strong," the old woman warned. It went on that way for days which turned into weeks and, as Dadou refused to eat, over time his body became very thin and weak. All of Dadou's songs were now filled with sadness as he sat locked up in the old woman's hut.

"Dadou, such sad songs you now sing!" the old woman would scold. Eventually, the little bird was no longer strong enough to sing and his music was no longer heard. All of the villagers and the animals began to wonder what happened to the great voice of the once lively little bird who had filled their days with joy. How they missed those beautiful sounds.

"He died of sadness!" the villagers would gossip.

The old woman, too, missed the happy sounds of the once happy Dadou. She realized that it was she who caused his sounds to cease and so she set about healing him. She had to first allow him to accompany her on her walks through the forest again which was his favorite activity.

"Dadou, would you come with me into the forest again," she asked him. His eyes sparkled at the invitation yet he was too weak to move and the old woman carried him in her harvesting satchel.

After their walks, when the woman and Dadou would return to the hut, the little bird enthusiastically ate his favorite soup that the woman would prepare for him.

Each day, Dadou grew stronger and soon his body was strong enough to sing and once more his joyous songs graced the skies. The villagers and the forest animals were very grateful to have the beautiful sounds fill their days again.

The time had come for Dadou to leave and, this time, the old woman knew she had to let him go.

"Dadou, my friend, it is time for you to return to your life and to your own home. I cannot keep you here any longer." Although sad to be leaving his friend, the little bird was happy at the thought of being able to fly high in the skies and to journey back to his village.

With tears in her eyes, the old woman gently patted Dadou on the head and placed him on the open window sill. Dadou turned to look one last time at the old woman who had taken him from the forest floor and smiled. Then he launched himself up and out into the world. Free at last, his beautiful song floated down into the forest trees below and up, up, up into the sky.

OTHER BOOKS BY THE AUTHOR

After The Darkness: A survivor's TRUE story of childhood incest, rape, abuse, domestic violence, and her ability to overcome the negative impact these events had on her life. (2018)

Born Different: A Woman's Spiritual Journey of Self-Acceptance (2019)

Today, I Feel Ugly: Overcoming Negative Self-Image (2019)

The Rainbow Ribbon (2019)

Cuddly Cat (2020)

Moon Child (2019)

Running Waters: The Poetry of A Woman's Soul (2010)

Blessed Pleasures: The Sensuality of A Woman (2010)
Musings of a Woman (2022)

Visit www.candacenadinebreen.com to contact the author, to learn more about the author and for more work by the author!

ABOUT THE AUTHOR

Candace Nadine Breen is of West African (Nigeria, Benin, Cameroon of the Yoruba and Fulani tribes) descent and wears many hats.

She taught English in Providence, Rhode Island for eleven years for grades seven and nine. During that time, she tried to find her place in society while being driven away from various religious organizations for her inability to conform to their standards.

While raising a family, she returned to school and earned a Master's in Human Services with a focus on Marriage and Family Counseling. She was later a real estate agent for a few years but found it unfulfilling ,stressful and time consuming. After taking time to open up herself to her true path, she buried herself in metaphysical studies, earning a Master's of Science and Doctorate in Metaphysics.

She became a Spiritualist Minister which seemed like the perfect occupation for her, at first, but she gradually felt that she was outgrowing the Spiritualist community and was told by a medium unknown to her that her path would not end with the Spiritualist Church. She is now a Metaphysical Minister.

It was very difficult for Candace to fit into societal boxes and , after, falling into depression, she threw caution to the wind and decided to follow her true calling. She embraced her psychic talents, wrote and published three successful memoirs, threw herself into her art and began working on children's books, young adult fiction books and sci-fi novels.

Candace is a Master Gardener and has always loved gardening and just being outside in nature. She has found satisfaction in earth-based religions and solitary spiritual practices despite the fact that she refuses to be labeled as any particular religion. She enjoys being in her garden, meditating in her wooded and quiet backyard, painting, art, and spending time with her family. She studies earth magick, gives Spirit messages via intuitive tarot reading, runes, herbal medicine and her mediumship abilities.

Candace also devotes herself to speaking, helping and healing for the highest and greatest good. She hosts the podcast “It’s All Good: Magick, Mysticism & Earth Medicine”. She is also an initiate to the Mami Wata Spirit.

Candace currently resides in Barrington, Rhode Island.

www.ingramcontent.com/pod-product-compliance
Lightning Source LLC
LaVergne TN
LVHW010112170826
845678LV00012B/2371
* 9 7 9 8 3 5 2 7 5 5 8 3 9 *